Especially for
Lina, Vince, Catherine, & Craig

CIP Data is available.

Published in the United States 2000 by Dutton Children's Books,
a division of Penguin Putnam Books for Young Readers
345 Hudson Street, New York, New York 10014
http://www.penguinputnam.com/yreaders/index.htm

Originally published in Great Britain 1999 by Methuen Children's Books,
an imprint of Egmont Children's Books Limited, London
Printed in Hong Kong   First American Edition
ISBN 0-525-46213-9
2 4 6 8 10 9 7 5 3 1

RED'S GREAT CHASE

by

Simone Lia

Dutton Children's Books
New York

**Red tiptoed into the dark basement.
She hugged her blue bunny.**

You never know when a scary monster
might jump out, she thought.

Just then, she saw one!

The scary monster started to chase Red

up the stairs

out of the house

down **the** **path**

past the stores

over the hill

along the winding road

into the park

through the jungle

under the ground

→ **up a tall building**

across the blue mountains

until Red was all out of breath.

"Gotcha!"

the scary monster roared.
"And now it's . . .

. . . your turn to chase me, Red!"